Jack Dann has written or edited
ing the international bestselle
The Rebel, The Silent, Bad Medicine, and The Man Who Melted. His work has been compared to Jorge Luis Borges, Roald Dahl, Lewis Carroll, Ray Bradbury, J. G. Ballard, Mark Twain, and Philip K. Dick. Library Journal called Dann "...a true poet who can create pictures with a few perfect words," and Best Sellers said that "Jack Dann is a mind-warlock whose magicks will confound, disorient, shock, and delight."

He is a recipient of the Nebula Award, the World Fantasy Award (twice), the Australian Aurealis Award (three times), the Chronos Award, the Darrell Award for Best Mid-South Novel, the Ditmar Award (five times), the Peter McNamara Achievement Award and the Peter McNamara Convenors' Award for Excellence, the Shirley Jackson Award, and the Premios Gilgames de Narrativa Fantastica award. He has also been honored by the Mark Twain Society (Esteemed Knight).

His latest novel is *Shadows in the Stone: a Book of Transformations*. New York Times bestselling author Kim Stanley Robinson called it "such a complete world that Italian history no longer seems comprehensible without his cosmic battle of spiritual entities behind and within every historical actor and event." Dr. Dann is also an Adjunct Senior Research Fellow in the School of Communication and Arts at the University of Queensland. He lives in Australia on a farm overlooking the sea.

IFWG Publishing's Chapbook Series of Titles

Black Moon: Graphic Speculative Flash Fiction, by Eugen Bacon

Tool Tales: Microfiction Inspired by Antique Tools, by Kaaron Warren (photography by Elen Datlow)

Stark Naked (poetry collection) by Silvia Cantón Rondoni

Infectious Hope: Poems of Hope and Resilience From the Pandemic, edited by Silvia Cantón Rondoni

Morace's Story (children's novella, companion to Walking the Tree) by Kaaron Warren

Songs From a White Heart (poetry collection), by Jack Dann

An IFWG Publishing Chapbook

Songs From a White Heart

A Poetry Collection
by Jack Dann

Songs From a White Heart

ISBN-13: 978-1-922556-97-4

V1.0

The contents' history can be found at the end of this collection.

Printed in Palatino Linotype and FreightNeo Pro.

IFWG Publishing International

www.ifwgpublishing.com

Table of Contents

Acknowledgements

The author would like to thank the following people for their support, aid, and inspiration:

Jenny Blackford, Russell Blackford, Mike Foldes, Robert Frazier, my publisher Gerry Huntman, Stephen Jones, Tappan King, Charles and Betty Ann Kochis, Gillian Polack, Udo Schuklenk, Jeanne Van Buren, Karen Van Kleeck, Gill and Deborah Williams; and, as always, my partner Janeen Webb.

For Albert White and Jim Holley…
And for Joseph Lindsley, who started it all:
Rest in peace, dear friend.

Introduction

In 1978 I was in a sweat-lodge being led by a Sioux medicine man who, it was claimed, had the gift of eagles. It was explained to me that that was his medicine, his power. In that sweat-lodge where it was so hot that your skin could suddenly crack, I remember the steam coming up so hot that it actually felt cold[1]; I remember trying to hunker down into my blanket, and in that moment of sensory deprivation, in the intense heat and darkness, in that small space with eight other men…a space that seemed like miles of darkness…I heard a giant bellows working, felt something flapping inside the lodge, felt the touch of feathers, as something very large frantically flew about, trying to get out of that dark.

The bellows was probably my own blood pounding. The medicine man had an eagle's wing, and was slapping it against my thigh, probably

1 Temperatures as high as 140 to 170 degrees Fahrenheit have been reported in sweat-lodges; and, indeed, I've seen people's skin blister from the heat.

waving the wing in the steam-black air. I know that now, knew it then; but I remember that on one level, it was an eagle loose in the sweat-lodge. I knew it was a trick, but a trick played by the Trickster, one that had resonance on a level beyond the rational. For in that instant I had felt the eagle, not the medicine man's feathers, but the eagle.

And I remember shyly asking someone who had sat next to me if he had felt anything strange in that session. He laughed and said, "Yeah, you mean the eagle in the sweat-lodge."

These poems comprise, in a sense, an autobiography of my experiences with traditional Native American religion. They seemed to 'write themselves,' and became part of that intense, joyous, fearful, and compacted time. But it should be understood that they are simply the thoughts, fears, notes, and musings of a middle-class white who had made a foray out of his culture.[2] They do not purport to lay open or accurately record Native American Sioux ceremonies. Traditional Native American religion is not often accessible

2 During that initial white hot time of exploration and revelation, I asked a medicine woman to vet the early poems that now make up the spine of this book. I had wanted to publish them in magazines and literary quarterlies, but did not feel comfortable doing so without her permission. She read the poems…and gave me her blessing. And over the long years that followed—long after I had lost touch with those who conducted and participated in the ceremonies I describe—I continued to write poems for this book. I alone take responsibility for any cultural gaffes and infelicities that these later poems might contain.

to non-Native Americans, and I've been told that most accounts of Native American religion are not entirely accurate. That is not to say that Native American culture is completely closed to outsiders, for it surely isn't. Many young whites are in fact living traditional Native American lifestyles. Most traditional Native Americans are, however, wary of 'Wannabees,' i.e., groupies who see Native American life as glamorous and want to be close to it.

I became involved with Native American religion as a result of a book I was researching, but I would be remiss if I didn't confess that some of these experiences, which are detailed in these poems, took on the form of a spiritual quest. I participated in the rights of Hanblecheyapi (the vision quest), Inipi (the sweat lodge), and the ceremonies of praying with the pipe and giving flesh; but my experiences in the sweat-lodge pervade the poems, so much so that I considered calling the chapbook Sweat-lodge Poems. I hope the sense of mystery and the transcendent fire of the sweat-lodge come through in these poems. And I hope that what might seem to be a change of heart at the end doesn't spoil the magic of what came before.

To my mind, it all partakes of the numinal!

Although the events that prompted these poems seem far away to me now, that time subtly changed the way I experience the world. I recall being at a friend's vision-quest where everyone was 'giving flesh,' a ceremony in which the medicine man cuts the supplicant's skin with a razor and drops the tiny pieces of flesh into a colored square of cloth, which the participant later ties to the branch of a near-by tree as a totem. I asked the medicine man why people were doing this, and he looked at me as if I had just asked the most stupid question imaginable. He laughed and answered, "Because that's the only thing you've got to give. Your skin is the only thing you really own. So you give a little of it to your friend, to help him. You give a little of yourself. You take a little pain for him."

And so I gave flesh.

For my partner. For my stepson. For my friend Albert. For all of us. And for a little while I lost hold of my ego. There and in the sweat lodge where I burned for a few minutes, or a few hours, I had the revelation—or aberration—depending on your point of view, that perhaps down deep in the quick of our unconscious our basic impulses are not selfish and self-seeking.

Of course, back then I also felt the wings of eagles beating in the sweat-lodge.

But that was a long time ago…

Telescope

NOW IT'S A telescope
now a dark well, and
we look back through
the sacred pipe,
through the skin-soaking
sweat-lodges and
stone fires,
through the spirits
flickering in the round
eternities
as we scream
and pray
and huddle for cover.

There, bright specks in the
matté memory darkness,
it's only us
wailing and
giving flesh
before evaporating into
hotcold steam.

Now we're the film clips
the movies
the ghost-flickering frames
the sounds echoing in
the empty selfish galleries
as the medicine man carves
bloody lines down our arms
cuts our foreheads, our shanks,
thighs, buttocks.

We're old meat,
but we're also
razor blades
shimmering glinting
cutting red prayers
for our families
and friends
and enemies all
metal, bone and flesh.

In the movies we're
all walking in procession
children, adults,
witches, warlocks, mages,
prestidigitators,
bad-medicine makers
carrying the earth and star gifts
to the one who would stand
on the hill and perhaps
find his name
his vision
his mission and glory
Amen.

But we know
what we were
phonies and actors and
saints and wannabees
pretending so hard that
for a while, for those leaf
and yellow days and weeks,
we became the natural people
the red and white
two-leggeds living earth lives
dying and returning
through the dark cold tunnel
the well
the other end of the telescope

We Sat in the Sweat-Lodge

WE SAT IN the sweat-lodge
Just Albert and I
and others kept the door
to pass in coals and water
but they were in the world
and we were in the round
darkness.

A hot sweat, the steam
cold as winter telephone
lines, and Albert had to
push me into the mud-sticky
ground, into the warm
breathing earth,
to still my screams.

And he prayed in the spaces
of time I lost
too compressed
in my own pain
to listen.

Except I remember
even now…

When the flaps were raised
so we could rest
and breathe
he said,
"We're too old,
we're past the time
to be warriors."

Yet then my hair was brown
not gray, and my face
was not my father's
as it is now.
And I didn't know then
the ancient pain I would
feel again
and once again.

I dream of that sweat-lodge,
except there I sit
in the fever of middle-age
wasting toward goals
built out of paper
and ink.

In that spirit-dream
I hold a telephone,
that rings in the
suffocating darkness
the office I've become.
And a friend calls
and tells me that
a child has died.

The rocks are red hot
and the steam is white
and I scream for my friend
for my child
for myself.

But before I can hang up
and wrap myself in the blanket
the phone rings once again

Rings in my hand
as if it's
a plastic appendage
that the years have grown.

And another voice,
my wife,
tells me that I
must make a new prayer
for another death.

Now I burn here
in the darkness
of my youth and middle-age
and once again I scream
and press my face
into the sweat moistened mud.

Afraid…

A child
afraid to look up and see
the flickering spirits
afraid
to watch them

turn into darkness
one by one and
leave me to my own
selfish, foolish thoughts
of ancient and eternal
night.

A Good Day to Die

IT WAS A good day to die
A good day to sweat
A good day to pray
A good day to be with friends
A good day to be alone on the hill
And vision quest

Nerve

"ALBERT," I SAY
"I feel hot."
He looks at me
questioning.

"Like a wire," I say
and he nods. "I
feel sweaty and removed
from the world."

He sits down beside me
and promises not to let the
others take me when I
fall off the edge.

"No hospitals," I say
"No institutions no electric
shocks, I'm already hot."
"No shocks," he says and makes a prayer.

So I fall. And find a feather in
my hair. Through layers of gauze, I see

him walking me like a dog about to
be made-into stew.
Then he sweats my body in the lodge
and takes it-not-I to the hill
where the visions wait.
And there I meet myself.

The Ground Has a Face

THE GROUND HAS a face
Yellow with autumn today

The trees make a grotto.
The ties on the sweat-lodge are red

We smoke the pipe
Pipestone red as the ties

The smoke rises to the four directions
We pull for the spirits and exhale the
light

Great Mystery

OH, WAKAN TANKA
Make it hard

Make it hard in our sweat lodge
Make it hard on our vision quests

Let our bones melt in the steam
and fragrant sweat of prayer

Oh, Great Mystery
We want to live

It Is a Circle

IT IS A circle.
Albert sweats me
and cuts my flesh.
We smoke the pipe
and I embrace him
and leave him to
the hill to vision
quest. All the
dreams like children
growing as I watch
my companion become
a medicine man.

A good dream, this
circle. But had we
known how dark it
could he, had we known
the terrors and the
wreckage, the losses
and longing, would
we have dreamed this
circle
?

Ceremony

I BURN IN the darkness
with the others. I
fold into my sweat-stinking
blanket

My body hot wax my hair
on fire. I look down
at the rock people glowing
before me.

Steam chokes me, spirits
flicker in the round
blackness and I tell myself
I'm not afraid.

Oh, *Wakan lanka,* what is
this Jew-boy doing here
burning for a vision
in the sweat lodge?

The Medicine Man

THE MEDICINE MAN tells me
I will not die
and shouts for his people
so they may live.

He calls the eagle
and I feel its feathers
and the beating of the world
as I breathe.

My insides are bellows
for the spirits touching
me with feathers of their
sweat-soaked dream.

I Died for a While

I DIED FOR a while
and rode the black and

silver and saw the spirits
and found the visions

and sang the songs. I
found my name. I lost

myself in the dark where
no one could help me.

I found nothing but voices
and the eagles that

flew in the sweat-lodge
for the spirits.

An Old Man's Poem

And lastly
an old man's poem
a prayer

Perhaps
a resolution

for an old
wannabe
atheist

OH, I'VE LOOKED for you…

As a child I intoned my prayers before bedtime with invocatory repetition (*"Here-oh-Israel-the-Lord-our-God-the-Lord-is-one"*). I sat in moist, old-man-smelling synagogues on holy days beside my father (and still, even now, the phrase "May he rest in peace" echoes through my tunnels and labyrinths of memory). I dutifully searched for the elusive spirit, the divine presence, what kabbalists call the *shekhinah*. I searched other religions, meditated, and squatted in Native American sweat-lodges so hot that it cracked open skin. I've screamed for a vision, felt and heard eagles breathing me in and breathing me out in the edgy darkness that was so hot it felt cold. I've eaten raw heart, seen medicine men put hot coals in their mouths, learned ancient Hebrew, studied the Torah, practiced lucid dreaming, found my way into monochromatic hallucinations of height, and almost fell off those vertiginous psychedelic cliffs.

I knew then in the hot, hormonal summer of youth, just as I know now in the cooler and more comfortable winter of senior citizenship, that there was no eagle in that sweat-lodge, even though other men felt its presence as I did. I had rationalized the experience as consensual hallucination, but even while I felt the flapping and brushing of wings—even as the sweat-lodge itself became a huge bellows—I *knew* that the medicine man was shaking and waving an eagle's feather, beating it against my skin. I *knew* that the bellows was my own breathing. I *knew* that the extreme heat, the complete darkness—the sensory deprivation—the searing hot/cold pain had put me into an altered state in which I imagined—and, yes, experienced—epiphanies. In those knife-edged instants I imagined that I grasped essential meanings (forgotten seconds after), felt the numinal presence of the *shekhinah,* and experienced the "word made flesh"...

Once, during a break from writing a novel, I paced through my house in upstate New York.

The house had been built before the Civil War and the windows caught the light, which pooled in various rooms throughout the day. As I walked from room to room, window to window, I suddenly experienced a heightened focus, an existential moment. I felt that I was looking at the familiar with new eyes, and I realized at the time that this sense of euphoria, this realization of the enchantment of the mundane, was a gift that would last but a few minutes. Which it did, yet for those few moments *"the house-roofs seemed to heave and sway, the church-spires flamed, such flags they had,"* to borrow from Robert Browning.

Yes, I looked for you…

I looked for you in the shadows of grief and in the molten early-morning Sabbath light as I sat with friends in the synagogue. I looked for you as youth gave way to middle age and I called myself an agnostic. I was willing to follow the mystics' 'way of the fool'; and so the years passed. And only now that my hair has faded from gray to white, now that I see a stranger with a high-boned wrinkling face in the mirror, now that I am no longer a 'warrior' lit by adrenaline and testosterone…and now that the ever-increasing weight of mortality is constant, I call myself an atheist. After all the sweat-lodges, synagogues, and churches, after all the study and meditation, after most of a life surrounded by books, by philosophy, theology, history, science, and that miraculous means of transport—fiction; I find myself alone with my thoughts. The *'you'* I desperately searched for was...*me*. How I yearned to connect with something larger than myself. How I yearned for moments of consuming bliss. I yearned for peace and security, and an intercessory God who could be propitiated with prayer and sacrifice. But as we witnessed in the Nazi concentration camps and the killing fields of Cambodia, all the prayers, spells, and supplications in the world can't save us from the terrible deeds of our fellow men. Perhaps we might hope in education, technology, and science. Perhaps a rigorous rational exploration of our psyches and the universe might help us conquer the beast and evolve into more rational beings. But I suppose that, too is a prayer…a supplication. An irrational hope.

I've found some modicum of peace and security, but I just couldn't push myself into belief. I've tried to expand my consciousness into altered states; I've tried to believe that those precious moments of heightened consciousness came from without rather than from within; and I've tried to find some evidence of a personal god. I can appreciate the complexity, beauty, dignity, and artful harmonies of the world's great belief systems, just as I can enjoy the breathtaking architectural elegance of philosophical ideas such as Leibnetz's *Monadology*. Some of these systems are often almost mathematically consistent internally, but they all require leaps of faith I am not willing to make. And as I approach my own mortality, Pascal's wager and all the other anti-rational, anti-scientific rationalizing have come to ring more and more hollow.

I've had luminous moments when I can see more deeply…and hope to have more. I've seen the magic in the everyday…and hope to see more.

So herewith, tongue cleaving to cheek, is an atheist's prayer:

I hope to explore all the demons, ghosts, angels, and hobgoblins of my psyche; I hope to explore the limits of thought and possibility; I hope to embrace humankind's daily discoveries in art, science, and technology; and I will only blame myself and ourselves for the errors, petty cruelties, holocausts, wars, and killing fields of the past, present, and future. I will reject the safety of teleology. I will not pray for redemption. I will not rail at the gods. I will not beseech. I will not embrace superstition and irrationality to overcome my fears of death and uncertainty. And I will continue to peer into the deep well of mortality and try not to run because I am frightened.

Amen…

Or as the Sioux say: *Washtay*.

Acknowledgements

"Introduction" First published in different form as "A Gift of Eagles" in *Dancing With the Dark: True Encounters With the Paranormal by Masters of the Macabre,* edited by Stephen Jones, 1997.

"Telescope" First published in *Baggage,* edited by Gillian Polack, 2010.

"We Sat in the Sweat-Lodge" Original to this anthology.

"A Good Day to Die" First published in *Rod Serling's The Twilight Zone,* August 1987.

"Nerve" First published in *Rod Serling's The Twilight Zone,* August 1987.

"The Ground Has a Face" First published in *The Anthology of Speculative Poetry 4,* 1980.

"Great Mystery" First published in *Rod Serling's The Twilight Zone,* August 1987.

"It is a Circle" First published in *Rod Serling's The Twilight Zone,* August 1987.

"Ceremony" First published in *The Anthology of Speculative Poetry 4,* 1980.

"The Medicine Man" First published in *Rod Serling's The Twilight Zone,* August 1987.

"I Died for a While" First published in *The Anthology of Speculative Poetry 4,* 1980.

"An Old Man's Poem" First published in different form as "Antinomies" in *50 Voices of Disbelief,* edited by Russell Blackford and Udo Schuklenk, 2009